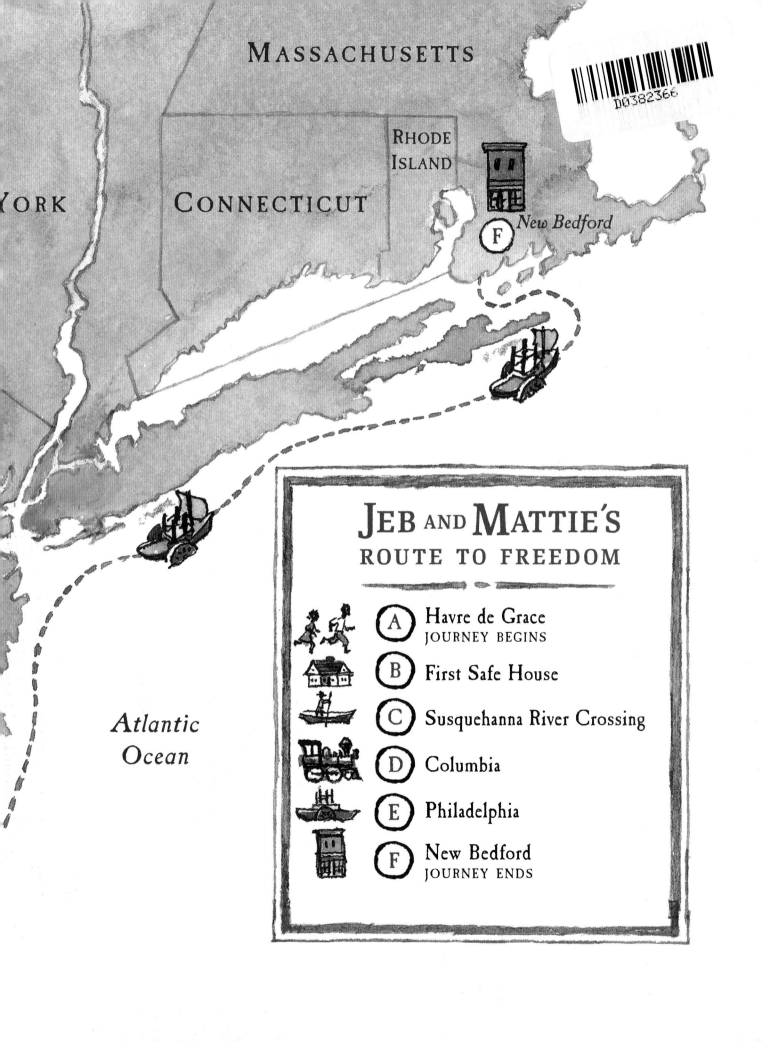

MASSACHUSETTS

RHODE
ISLAND

YORK

CONNECTICUT

New Bedford

F

Atlantic
Ocean

JEB AND MATTIE'S
ROUTE TO FREEDOM

(A) Havre de Grace
JOURNEY BEGINS

(B) First Safe House

(C) Susquehanna River Crossing

(D) Columbia

(E) Philadelphia

(F) New Bedford
JOURNEY ENDS

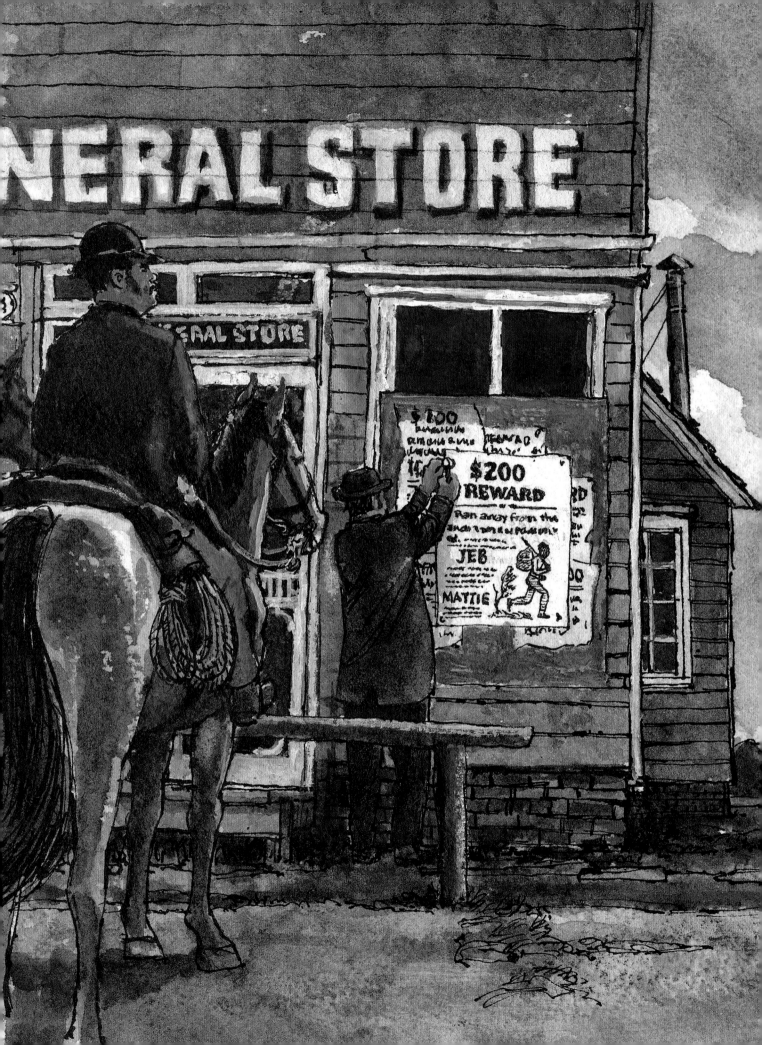

...S · FROM · THE
UNDERGROUND RAILROAD

by KAY WINTERS · illustrated by LARRY DAY

DIAL BOOKS FOR YOUNG READERS

DIAL BOOKS FOR YOUNG READERS • *Penguin Young Readers Group*
An imprint of Penguin Random House LLC • 375 Hudson Street, New York, NY 10014

Text copyright © 2018 by Kay Winters • Illustrations © 2018 by Larry Day

Printed in China • ISBN 9780803740921 • 10 9 8 7 6 5 4 3 2 1
Designed by Jason Henry • Text set in Caslon Antique
The artwork for this book was created with pencil, pen and ink with watercolor and gouache on watercolor paper.

JEB

:::: ✕ ::::

TONIGHT'S THE NIGHT.
    My sister Mattie passed me the word.
The auctioneer's comin'.
We gotta go.
Leave Maryland.
Run to freedom like our brother Ben
before it's too late.

I used to be a field hand,
but now I'm hired out to the blacksmith in town.
I work hard but get no pay.
The master collects it.

I have a friend, Samuel, who works there.
He's free.
He's got papers that say so.
Samuel's part of the Underground Railroad,
folks who help slaves go North.
He told me how to find his place
and promised to help when we was ready to run.

The master'll sell me South just like he did Mama
to help pay his gambling debts.
Mama made Mattie and me promise we'd go.
I still see her face. Hear her wails.
Hear that gavel bang . . . SOLD!

        Ain't gonna happen.
        Not again.
        Not to me. Not to Mattie.
        Not gonna be sold like a pig or a plow.
        We gotta run.

MATTIE

It's time. . . . We *have* to run.
I heard the missus talk about the auction.
She said Jeb's name.
Maybe me as well.
Who knows? We can't wait and see.

Folks say I'm lucky to be a house slave.
Those folks have never been one.
Missus screams at me, slaps me, hits me with a poker
if the baby fusses, the twins won't mind,
or the Master loses again . . . gambling.
I'm scared of him. Such a temper!
Never know what he'll do next.

I clean the fireplaces,
empty the slop, mind the children.
The baby Caroline sleeps through the night now.
I sleep on the floor next to her cradle.
The twins have their own room.
    I can slip away.

No one will miss me till morning.
I'll miss the baby, so sweet and soft.
She smiles for me.
Only one who does.
       But that's all I'll miss!
          Never a kind word.
           Always afraid.
             I want to be free!

WE GOTTA GO.

JEB

MATTIE MADE IT!
I feared somebody'd hear her.
We got no map, but there's the North Star
just like Mama said.
   If we get lost we'll follow that star.

We slip and slide, up slopes and down,
scramble through brush, duck low limbs,
dodge branches, climb over logs,
listen for footsteps following
or dogs howling.

Whoo whoo who . . . . Mattie clutches me.
My heart lurches. I look around.
Just a hoot owl, I say.

   Never been off the place before, Mattie mutters.
   What if we get caught like Julian?
   Brought back in chains.
   Beaten till his back bled.
   Then he had to wear that iron rack
   with bells on his head.

   Can't think about Julian, I say.
   Think about Ben.
   He got away. Got to New Bedford.
   That's where we're going.
   I miss Ben, Mattie says.
   I loved to hear him whistle!
   Remember Hush Little Baby?

Oh . . . We're here, Samuel's house! I tell Mattie.

   I rap three times.
   And hope.

SAMUEL
·CONDUCTOR·

SOMEONE'S KNOCKING.
Someone in trouble.

I peer through the glass.
It's Jeb and his sister!
    You're going! I say.
I open the door
and hurry them in.
My wife shuts the curtains.
    Sit down. I'll get you something to eat.

    We had to go, Jeb explains.
    They was gonna sell me South.
    I wasn't leaving Mattie behind.

    Soon as you've eaten,
    I need to move you on, I tell them.
    We're watched by bounty hunters.
    Not safe to keep you here for long.
    I'll take you to the nearest station.

    What's a station? asks Mattie.
    It's a safe place to hide folks, I say.
    We use railroad words as a kind of code.

    Amos might be next, Jeb says.
    When he came into the blacksmith yesterday
    he said his Master died and he might have to run.

    Have you moved many on? Jeb asks.
    About thirty, I tell them.
    What happens if you get caught?
    Jail, I say. *And a fine, maybe worse.*

My wife puts out hot tea, bread, and slices of ham.
                 We eat and then we go.

CLARINDA
· MISTRESS OF OAKLAND ·

GONE! I SHRIEK. *MATTIE'S GONE....*
The baby's wet, and hungry.
Quiet!! thunders my husband, Seth,
and gives me a swat.
If Mattie's run, Jeb's run, too. I'll go see.

I'm Missus of Oakland.
Papa left the house and the slaves to me.
But then I married Seth.
Didn't know he's a gambler, has a filthy temper, and likes the ladies.
Now we have to have an auction to pay off his debts.

Gone, says Seth as he comes back with Flint, our overseer.
Blast their black hides!
They've run away just like their brother Ben.
Slave catchers will get 'em, says Flint.
Look at Julian. We caught him!

All the slaves saw what you did to Julian, I say.
And still they run.
Wait till these two feel my one hundred lashes, says Flint.
His eyes glitter.
He snaps his whip.
They're my property, says Seth.
And it was mine, I say to myself.
The two of them would have brought $500.

I'll hire slave catchers, put out an ad, says Seth,
then go to that blacksmith where Jeb worked.
Those two can't have gotten far.

Maybe the blacksmith heard something, I say.
Or maybe he hides them hisself, sneers Flint.

ELIJAH
·STATIONMASTER·

TAP TAP TAP.
"Who's there?" I call softly.
A friend with friends, comes the reply.
I open the door to a young lad and a girl,
hurry the pair in, and sit them in the kitchen.
Samuel slips away.

> *Thee is welcome,* my wife says.
> *But it won't be long till folks know*
>   *thee is gone.*
> *Follow me,* I say.

I take up a rug,
lift three floorboards and beckon.
> *This is thy hiding place.*
> *There are pallets on the floor for sleeping.*

The girl gasps. . . . I hand her a lantern.
> *It's dark there, but safe,* I tell her.
The two grope their way
down the stone staircase
to the root cellar below.
> *Rest now,* I say.
> *We'll eat and talk later.*

That afternoon my son Thomas and I
go out to the barn,
saddle my horse, and ride into town.
There they are!
Slave catchers.
An abomination to mankind.
They're posting an ad in the window of the general store.

We keep riding.

BLACKSMITH
·OPERATIVE·

THE DOOR TO MY BLACKSMITH SHOP OPENS.
Three men stride in.
It's Seth, owner of Oakland,
with slave catchers, Rufus and Angus.
I know them well.

> *Good afternoon,* I say.
> *What can I do for you?*

> *Looking for my property.*
> *Jeb, and his sister Mattie,* says Seth.
> *You know Jeb. He worked here.*
> *He and his sister have run off,*
> *just like their brother before them.*
> *You hear anything? See them?*
> *Or are they hidden here?* says Angus.
> *We know free coloreds hide slaves.*

> *I haven't seen them.*
> *You are welcome to look,* I say calmly.

The men stomp around the forge,
where the fire burns and the smoke rises.
I follow them to the barn.
They stab the hay with a pitchfork,
stride out to the stables, check the stalls.
> *We'll be watching,* says Angus.
> *We always get 'em,* says Rufus
And the two ride off.

Samuel must have moved them on . . .
I'll get word to Elijah.
The hunt's begun!

JEB

W E'VE BEEN HERE WITH THE QUAKERS
for three days now.
These folks hid us, fed us,
gave us different clothes.
I work in the barn with their son Thomas.
Mattie helps with the baby.

> *Thee is so brave*, Thomas says.
> *I don't know if I could . . .*
> I say, *We've been lucky so far.*
> *Your father thinks it's time to move us on.*
> *Out of reach of those slave catchers.*

After supper the missus gives us both a sack of food.

> *For thy journey*, she says.
> *We'll never forget you*, Mattie says.
> *Godspeed*, she replies.

Thomas leads the way to the river.
A man is waiting in a flat-bottomed boat.

> *We're going across the Susquehanna*, he says.

Thomas gives me a smooth river stone.

> *For luck*, he says.

I gulp! I can't swim!
But I have to be brave for Mattie.
We get in the boat.
It tilts from side to side.
Off we go.

MATTIE

=== ·:· === æ === ·:· ===

AFTER THE CROSSING,
we start up the river,
keep close to the bank.
Now our guide rows more slowly . . . quietly.
It's s p o o k y dark.
We glide along.

Suddenly our conductor puts his finger to his lips.
       Voices! Up ahead!
I help slide the boat into the bushes.
We scramble up the bank,
hide in the brush.

A light flashes back and forth . . . .
          They're coming close.
             Closer. . . .

I can hardly breathe.
My hands are ice cold.
I grab Jeb's shirt,
shut my eyes, hold tight.
They must hear my heart hammering.
My chest feels like it will explode!

 Will they see us?
      Will they take us back??

ANGUS AND RUFUS
· SLAVE CATCHERS ·

This river's a highway for runaways, says Angus.
We caught four last week!

Dumb darkies, snorts Rufus.
They think they'll be safe once they get to Pennsylvania
cuz it's a free state.

We have to git that Jeb and Mattie
who ran from Oakland, Angus says.
They can't have gotten too far.

Their owner IS a mean one, says Rufus.
Beats his wife, cheats at cards.
Angus nods. Seth'll be wanting 'em back all right.
He needs the money.

Rufus swings the lantern so it shines
Up and down the river . . .
           Up and down . . . .

They couldn't just vanish, Angus says.
But their brother did, says Rufus.
We never found him.
Folks said he got on the Underground Railroad
        and disappeared . . . .

Well, this river's not underground.
If they're here, we'll catch 'em, vows Angus.
He stands up in the boat
shines the lantern
back and forth on the riverbank.
             Back and forth.
Nothing stirs . . . .
The only sound is the
        slap slap slap of the oars.

JEB

⋮⋮⋮ ═══════════ ✾ ═══════════ ⋮⋮⋮

TOO *RISKY ON THE RIVER RIGHT NOW,*
our guide says softly.
Follow the water. Keep away from the bank.
When you come to the stone house, knock.
They'll say, who goes there? You say, William Penn.
Our conductor disappears into the dark.

We pick our way along the river.
Brambles tear at our arms and faces.
    What's that? asks Mattie.
    SHHHH, I say. We crouch where we are.
I squeeze my lucky stone.
DOGS !!!!
I HATE DOGS!
Slave catchers sometimes use them to hunt fugitives.

We wait. We watch. We listen.
No voices . . . Just dogs growling and howling.
I whisper, *They hear us but I think they're penned.*
We walk slowly at first, then faster.

There it is! The stone house.
I knock and wait. . . .
    Who goes there?
    William Penn, I say.
A young girl leads us to the stable.
We sink into the hay and sleep.

The next morning a new conductor appears.
    Welcome to Pennsylvania, he says.
    We'll go in the Dearborn.
He points to a small carriage.
We climb up, he pulls the curtains and gets in the driver's seat.
We begin again.

CONDUCTOR
·STOCKHOLDER·

A DEARBORN PULLS INTO OUR LUMBERYARD.
Must be new parcels to go on the train.
A boy and girl step down.

Where're you headed? I ask the pair.
New Bedford, says the girl. *Our brother Ben is there.*
I'll send word to the Vigilance Committee
in Philadelphia, I say to them.
We'll get you there.
On a real railroad? the girl asks.
A real train. I smile.
We can hide you in a boxcar.

How many you helped escape? the boy asks.
Hundreds, I say. *I send some to Pittsburgh,*
and others to Philadelphia in our cars.
Last week we hid twelve.
Finally those no-goods left to look elsewhere.

We have to be more careful now, I say.
The new Fugitive Slave Law
forces everyone to help a constable and bounty hunters
capture runaways.

My nephew shows the two their secret compartment.
I get packages of food for the journey.
> *Safe travels,* I say.
> *Everyone should be free.*
I wish them well.

MATTIE

WE RIDE A LONG TIME.
     At last the train slows . . . then stops.
We inch out and look around.
A man is waiting with a wagon.
     He says, *New Bedford?* We nod.
He beckons. Big clay jars are in the wagon.
He pushes the straw aside,
slides open the false bottom.
Jeb and I climb into the opening.
It's dark in the hidey-hole. Hard to breathe.
We can hear him moving the jars over us.
We start off.

     HALT!!! comes a shout.
     Where are you going? asks a harsh voice.
     Philadelphia, our conductor says. *I'm taking the pottery there.*
     Look at all that straw! Let's see what's there, says one man.
     Straw protects the jars, our driver says.
I clutch Jeb. Don't let them find us. . . . Don't let them find us.
I say to myself again and again.

We hear the two climb up, kick the straw,
CRASH!!!
     You broke it! says the driver.
We barely breathe.

     Let's go, mutters one of the men.
     We'll be watching when you come back, says the other.
     $500 fine plus jail for helping a slave escape.

The wagon lurches and we start again.

JEB

æ

FINALLY WE STOP.
The board over our hidey-hole is lifted.
Philadelphia!
We uncurl and limp into an open back door.
A couple wait.

The woman says, *Welcome! Sit a spell and eat.*
You've had a long ride.
Your steamer will sail in two days.

Why New Bedford? the man asks.
Our brother Ben went last year, I say.
But we don't know where he lives.

We know others who have gone there, the man says.
We'll send word ahead . . . ask about Ben.
When you arrive go to Deacon Bush.
Turn left on Water Street. It's near the wharf.
He has a grocery store and a boardinghouse.
He and his wife help new arrivals.

Slave catchers don't tarry in that town, says the woman.
There's a liberty bell.
If trouble's brewing, folks ring that bell.
A big crowd appears, ready to fight.
Those bounty hunters flee!

Next day there's a tapping at the door.
Two women come in.
They hand us clean clothes, tickets for the steamship,
and an envelope with money.
From the Vigilance Committee
to help you get started in your new life.
A new life!
Think of it!

MATTIE

❖

EARLY IN THE MORNING WE GO TO
the Arch Street Wharf
where the steamship waits.
Our guide takes us to a crew member
who hurries us into the hold.
It's crowded with boxes, barrels, and freight.

Hide here till we leave port,
then you can come on deck, he says.
Bounty hunters sometimes board the ship when we stop.

The whistle blows.
In the distance we hear church bells chiming.
The steamship jolts, then glides forward.

At first the trip goes smoothly.
Sunny days follow one another.
We sleep on deck or on top of a trunk or a box in the hold.

Suddenly a storm comes up.
So does my supper.
The ship heaves from side to side.
Jeb and I go down to the hold.
Barrels roll, trunks slide, boxes crash.
Rain lashes the deck.
Thunder booms, lightning flashes.
The waves are high as houses.
I hold on so I won't slide into the sea.
There is no safe place to be.

I wonder . . . will we drown before we get there?

JEB

THE CREWMAN COMES. *New Bedford's next*, he says.
The ship pulls into Steamship Wharf.
We stumble off on wobbly legs.
A crowd waits.
We search the faces to find the one we know.
He isn't here.

> *Do you think we'll find him?* asks Mattie.
> *I hope so . . . At least we got here*, I say.
> *So many people helped*, Mattie says.
> *Samuel took us to Elijah.*
> *He sent us up the river.*
> *We hid from slave catchers. Rode a real railroad.*
> *Crammed into the hidey-hole in the wagon*, I add.
> *Sailed on the steamship from Philadelphia.*
> *And that storm! We made it through the storm!*

On Water Street we turn left
and watch for a grocery store.
Black people and white people are out and about.
No one looks afraid!

> But there's no sign of Ben.

Here's the store!

> *Jeb? Mattie?* asks the man behind the counter.
> *We got word you were coming.*
> *I'm Deacon Bush. Welcome to New Bedford!*
> *You'll be safe here*, adds his wife.

Suddenly we hear someone whistling—*Hush little baby . . .*
Could it be?
The door opens. *BEN! BEN!* we shriek.
You made it! Ben says,
from Maryland to Massachusetts.
Mama would be so proud!
Mrs. Bush smiles. *Come freshen up, have supper.*
We all want to hear your story.
And what a story it is!

HISTORICAL NOTES

❈

THE UNDERGROUND RAILROAD is the story of courageous freedom seekers who many times left the only place they had ever known, their friends and even families, to escape from their owners. Being enslaved was so degrading, so dehumanizing that many vowed they would rather die than return to that state of existence. Often they were helped by free blacks and concerned whites, as the runaways made their way to places where they believed they would be free. Many were successful. Some were not. Those who were caught were usually returned to their owners, and those who assisted were fined or jailed. The term Underground Railroad was more commonly used after the 1840s when the real railroad was in popular use, although aid was offered to escapees earlier than that. Terms such as conductor, station, passenger, stockholders, routes, and parcels were used as code. Underground implied secrecy.

WHY DID THE FREEDOM SEEKERS ESCAPE?

Enslaved persons had no rights. Most worked long hours with no pay, and had meager food. (Frederick Douglass in his autobiography tells of coarse cornmeal, tainted meat, children eating from a pig trough.) Many lived in shacks, slept on the floor, and were issued one or two sets of clothes per year. Those who lived on small farms were often hired out to work on neighboring plantations, at businesses in town, or on a nearby wharf. They were required to give the money they earned to their owner. Most were denied any sort of education. It was against the law to teach slaves to read. Many experienced frequent and brutal punishment. But the biggest fear of all was being "sold South," where conditions were reputedly much worse and they would be separated from family and friends.

WHO WAS MOST LIKELY TO RUN?

Those who lived in or near places that bordered on Free States had the greatest chance of escaping. Young men were the earliest travelers. Later, families ran as well.

HOW DID THEY GO?

Some walked. Others came partway on horseback or were hidden in wagons. Many came by ferry, canoe, rowboat, schooner, or steamer. They were taken on board by sympathetic captains, helped by black stewards, hidden in the hold, sometimes in barrels, trunks, or bales of cotton. Some did come on trains. Several even were shipped in boxes. Quite a few were disguised to mislead the bounty hunters. The Quaker bonnet and dress were sometimes used, as well as mourning clothes and veils. Occasionally, someone was transported in a coffin and became part of a funeral procession.

ROUTES

By 1850, there were hundreds of routes. Based on news of slave catchers in the area, conductors would choose the one that seemed safest. Often the guides would move back and forth between routes to throw hunters off the scent.

RAILROAD TERMINOLOGY

Station or *Safe House*: A place where it was safe to hide and wait. The time spent at a station depended on the circumstances. Often a stationmaster would keep his or her charges until the furor, public advertisements, or daily searching by bounty hunters had ceased. Sometimes they were sent on immediately. The stationmaster would secrete his guests in the basement, attic, spare room, root cellar, corncrib, icehouse, barn, or other outbuildings.

Although there are countless stories of tunnels and secret rooms, only a few of these accounts can be verified. Different clothes or disguises were often provided by a women's sewing group.

Conductor: Man or woman who took passengers from one location to another. Sometimes the guide led the way on foot. Other times the conductor was a driver of a carriage or cart, carrying a load of goods to deflect suspicion, or the rower of a boat, or captain of a ferry or steamboat. Harriet Tubman was a famous conductor. But unlike her, most conductors did not go back South; Most assisted those who were already on their way.

Operative: Go-between, someone in a central location who sent and received messages.

Stockholder: Person who supported the activities of those who were escaping with funding. Sometimes he or she physically assisted them. Other stockholders were only involved with funding.

Parcel: Code word for passenger. Often the number of travelers, ages, and sex were mentioned.

Abolitionist: Men and women who believed in the abolishment of slavery. Some were heavily involved in the Underground Railroad. Some served as stockholders, supplying funding to aid the traveler. Some served as stationmasters or conductors. They believed slavery to be wrong, and many ignored Federal laws to follow their conscience. They published newsletters to attract support and contributions. Meetings were held on local and regional levels. Speakers were brought in to describe the plight of the fugitive. Harriet Tubman, Frederick Douglass, Henry "Box" Brown, Ellen and William Craft shared their own experiences as chattel (human beings owned like property).

FUGITIVE SLAVE ACTS OF 1793 AND 1850

Both Federal laws provided for return of escaped black slaves between states.

1793– The law providing the return of fugitives was loosely enforced in the North to the frustration of the South. Many northern states passed personal-liberty laws that allowed a jury trial. Others passed laws forbidding state officials from helping to capture escaped slaves or put them in state jails.

1850– This law was passed to placate Southern slave-holding concerns and avoid Southern secession. More federal restrictions were added to permit slave hunters to capture a black person anywhere. They only had to tell a state or Federal judge that the person was a runaway. No proof required. A US Marshall who refused to return a runaway could be fined a thousand dollars. A person suspected of being a slave could be arrested without a warrant and turned over to the owner on testimony of ownership. A slave could not ask for a jury trial nor testify. According to Federal law, a free black, or any black, could not testify on behalf of anyone else. Anyone who assisted the runaway by providing shelter, food, or help of any kind was liable to six months in prison and five-hundred-dollar fine. Officers who captured a runaway slave received a fee, which encouraged some to kidnap free blacks and sell them to slave owners.

ROLE OF THE CHURCHES

Houses of worship played an important part in the Underground Railroad. Some churches became stations and hid freedom seekers. Others had members who served as conductors, stationmasters, or stockholders. African Methodist Episcopal churches and the Society of Friends were active participants. Some members from other denominations were also involved.

FINAL DESTINATIONS

Most freedom seekers went to Canada where they were legally free and welcomed by others who had gone before. Some settled in the communities they encountered as they fled Pennsylvania, Ohio, New York, Massachusetts, and other free states. But after the second Fugitive Slave Law was passed in 1850 it became easier for bounty hunters to kidnap their prey. Even free blacks were likely to be caught and sold. Many left their free states and fled to Canada. But others stayed and settled in communities like New Bedford, Massachusetts, where there was a large population of both free and fugitive blacks, a strong Quaker community, and a number of active abolitionists who saw slavery as a moral outrage. An escaping slave, George Teamoh, called the city the "Fugitives Gibraltar," because of the vigorous ways residents protected runaways. Slave catchers soon learned that it was hopeless to attempt recapture there. New Bedford was accessible by water and offered a variety of opportunities for employment to new arrivals. Although there was racial prejudice there, as there was in Canada, and objections were raised about new hires in some occupations, New Bedford became more than a stop on the Underground Railroad. It was a place where freedom seekers felt they could safely settle.

HISTORY REVISION

In recent years, revision of history regarding the Underground Railroad has taken place, as more information has emerged, and much more study has occurred from different and broader cultural viewpoints. Details of many escapes were not recorded for fear of hurting those who helped. Most early accounts were written by whites. Historians observe that runaways were often seen as helpless victims while their white helpers were described as heroes. But generalizations such as this are inaccurate. In 1850, after the second Fugitive Slave Law, some stationmasters who had kept records burned them. But William Still, a free black in Philadelphia, compiled an extensive record of some eight hundred escapes and those who made them. When danger of discovery threatened, he hid his records in a building loft in a cemetery until it was safe to retrieve them. Information about the blacks who participated in the Underground Railroad is continuing to emerge. Most freedom seekers who succeeded did so because of their own courage, determination, and flexibility to adjust quickly to changing circumstances. They were helped by whites, but many were also assisted by free blacks in communities, churches, as well as crew members on ships.

CONCLUSION

The Underground Railroad is a story of hope, hope for human beings who were being cruelly misused by other human beings. It is true that treatment of the enslaved varied. But in all cases, to consider people as property, like an animal or a table is unthinkable in this our "free land of liberty."

NOTE FROM THE AUTHOR

I became interested in the Underground Railroad when we moved to an old stone farmhouse in Quakertown, PA, built in 1800. I heard about Richard Moore, a teacher who became a potter, and was an active member of the local Society of Friends. Moore's house was an important station. Several times slave owners were at the potter's front door while their prey was slipping out the back. I heard Charles Blockson speak about his study of Underground Railroad activities in Pennsylvania. He described the Moore home as a major stop in Bucks County. Routes varied, of course, but I thought it possible that one of Moore's wagons, concealing runaways in the false bottom, redwood pots propped in straw on top, passed right by our farmhouse on the way to the next station.

My husband, Earl, and I went on our own journey beginning in Havre de Grace, Maryland, and ending in New Bedford, Massachusetts, before completing the book. We stayed in a bed and breakfast in Maryland, said to be a safe house during the 1800s. We were shown the secret passageway that led from the attic to the porch. We traveled to Berkley (or Darlington as it was called then), observed likely crossing spots on the Susquehanna River, and moved on to Columbia, Pennsylvania, where we went to a re-enactment sponsored by the local historical society. Here we were told about William Whipper (1804–1876), an African American entrepreneur who co-owned a railroad. Whipper had false boxcars created and some runaways rode a real train on their journey to freedom.

In New Bedford, Massachusetts, we were taken on a walking tour of Underground Railroad sites and heard about that community's role in creating a safe haven.

REFERENCES

Beims, Constance, Christine Tolbert. *A Journey Through Berkley, Maryland*. Baltimore, Maryland: Gateway Press, 2003.

Blockson, Charles L. *The Underground Railroad*. New York: Berkeley Publishing Group, 1987.

Douglass, Frederick. *The Complete Autobiographies of Frederick Douglass*. Radford, Virginia: Wilder Publications, 2008.

Foner, Eric. *Gateway to Freedom: Hidden History of the Underground Railroad*. New York, London: W. W. Norton and Co., 2015.

Gara, Larry. *The Liberty Line: the Legend of the Underground Railroad*. Lexington: University of Kentucky Press, 1961.

Grover, Kathryn. *The Fugitive's Gibraltar: Escaping Slaves and Abolitionism in New Bedford, Massachusetts*. University of Massachusetts Press, 2001.

Jordan, Ryan P. *Slavery and the Meetinghouse*. Bloomington and Indianapolis: Indiana University Press, 2007.

Kashatus, William C. *Just Over the Line: Chester County and the Underground Railroad*. Chester County Historical Society, 2002.

Leight, Robert L. *Richard Moore and the Underground Railroad at Quakertown*. Bedminster, PA: Adams Apple Press, 2006.

Northrop, Solomon. *Twelve Years a Slave*. Buffalo: Auburn, Derby and Miller, 1853.

Siebert, Wilbur H. *The Underground Railroad: From Slavery to Freedom*. New York: Macmillan, 1898.

Smedley, R. C. *History of the Underground Railroad in Chester and Neighboring Counties in Pennsylvania*. Lancaster, PA: Office of the Journal, 1883. Reprint. NY: Arno Press and the *New York Times*, 1969.

Still, William. *The Underground Railroad. A Record of Facts, Authentic Narratives, Letters*. Philadelphia: Porter and Coates, 1872.

Switala, William. *Underground Railroad in Pennsylvania*. Mechanicsburg, PA: Stackpole Books, 2001.

_____. *Underground Railroad in Delaware, Maryland and West Virginia*. Mechanicsburg, PA: Stackpole Books, 2004.

Thomas, Joseph D. and others. *A Picture History of New Bedford, Vol 1 1602–1925.* New Bedford: Spinner Publications, 2013.

BOOKS STUDENTS MIGHT ENJOY

Bial, Raymond. *The Underground Railroad.* Boston: Houghton Mifflin, 1995.

Bordewich, Fergus M. *Bound for Canaan. The Epic Story of the Underground Railroad.* New York: Harper Collins, 2005.

Clark, Margaret Goff. *Freedom Crossing.* New York: Scholastic, 1980.

Fradin, Dennis Brindell. *Bound for the North Star: True Stories of Fugitive Slaves.* New York: Clarion Books, 2003.

Fradin, Judith Bloom & Dennis Brindell Fradin. *The Price of Freedom: How one town stood up to slavery.* New York: Walker Books, 2013.

Landau, Elaine. *Fleeing to Freedom on the Underground Railroad: Courageous Slaves, Agents and Conductors.* Minneapolis: Twenty-First Century Books, 2006.

Lasky, Kathryn. *True North: A novel of the Underground Railroad.* New York: Blue Sky Press. Scholastic 1986.

Levine, Ellen. *If You Traveled on the Underground Railroad.* New York, Scholastic, 1993.

Malaspina, Ann. *The Underground Railroad: The Journey to Freedom.* New York: Chelsea House, 2010.

McDonough, Yona Zeldis. *What Was the Underground Railroad?* New York: Grosset & Dunlap, 2013.

ACKNOWLEDGMENTS

I would like to thank Irmgarde Brown, branch manager of Harford County Public Library in Havre de Grace, who introduced us to local sources of information and provided additional references. Randy Harris, historian, from the Columbia Historical Society who led the Underground Railroad tour and re-enactment. Lee Blake, president of the New Bedford Historical Society who spent several days with us, taking us on an Underground Railroad walking tour, showing us artifacts, and answering our questions.

Thanks also to the following authorities who kindly checked the book for historical and cultural accuracy: Herb Boyd, City College of New York; Ashley Jordan, Curator, National Underground Railroad Freedom Center, Cincinnati, Ohio; Kenneth S. Greenberg, Distinguished Professor, Department of History, Suffolk University, Boston, Massachusetts.

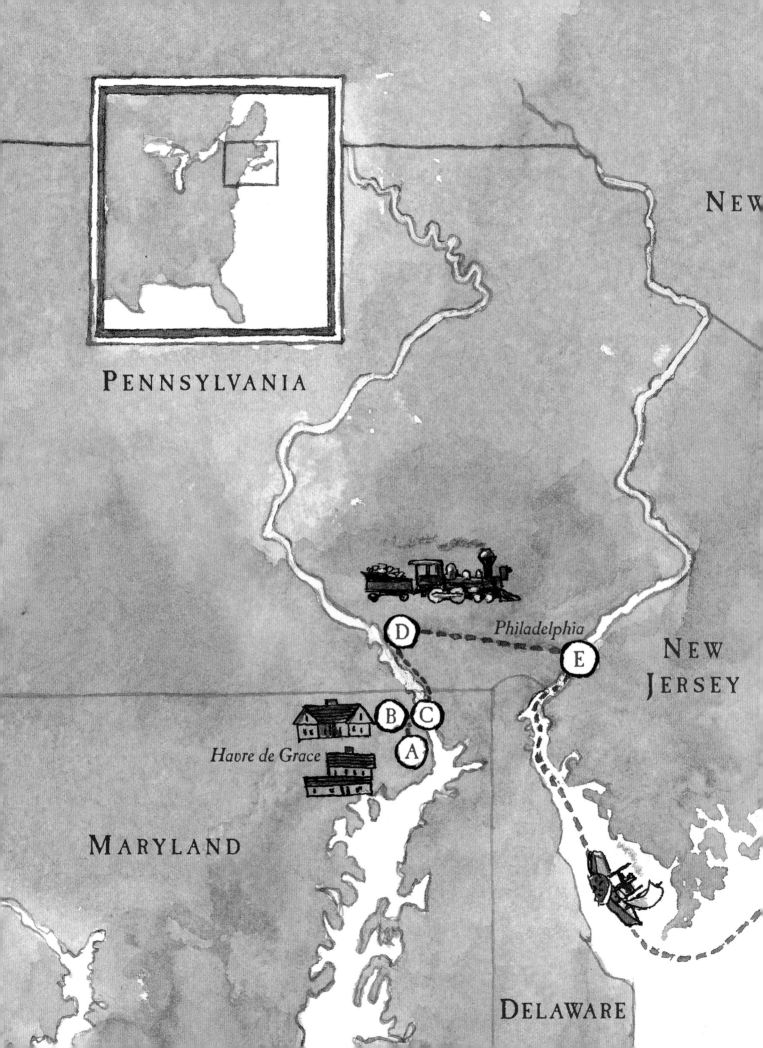

PENNSYLVANIA

NEW

NEW
JERSEY

Philadelphia

MARYLAND

Havre de Grace

DELAWARE